D0454846

Welcome Home!

Read all of
MARGUERITE HENRY'S Misty Inn
books!

#1 Welcome Home!
#2 Buttercup Mystery

And coming soon:

#3 Runaway Pony

Welcome home!

~~385237552~~

1ef   10/15/15

Misty's Inn

Welcome Home!

By Kristin Earhart

Illustrated by Serena Geddes

ALADDIN

New York London Toronto Sydney New Delhi

This book is a work of fiction. Any references to historical events, real people, or real places are used fictitiously. Other names, characters, places, and events are products of the author's imagination, and any resemblance to actual events or places or persons, living or dead, is entirely coincidental.

ALADDIN

An imprint of Simon & Schuster Children's Publishing Division

1230 Avenue of the Americas, New York, New York 10020

First Aladdin hardcover edition June 2015

Text copyright © 2015 by The Estate of Marguerite Henry

Illustrations copyright © 2015 by Serena Geddes

Also available in an Aladdin paperback edition.

All rights reserved, including the right of reproduction in whole or in part in any form.

ALADDIN is a trademark of Simon & Schuster, Inc., and the related logo is a registered trademark of Simon & Schuster, Inc.

For information about special discounts for bulk purchases, please contact Simon & Schuster Special Sales at 1-866-506-1949 or business@simonandschuster.com.

The Simon & Schuster Speakers Bureau can bring authors to your live event. For more information or to book an event, contact the Simon & Schuster Speakers Bureau at 1-866-248-3049 or visit our website at www.simonspeakers.com.

Designed by Laura Lyn DiSiena

The text of this book was set in Century Expanded.

Manufactured in the United States of America 0515 FFG

10 9 8 7 6 5 4 3 2 1

Library of Congress Control Number 2014958549

ISBN 978-1-4814-1414-2 (hc)

ISBN 978-1-4814-1413-5 (pbk)

ISBN 978-1-4814-1415-9 (eBook)

To my mom, who knows how to make
a place feel like home

Chapter 1

"WILLA, PLEASE STOP KICKING MY SEAT."

"Sorry, I didn't mean to," Willa Dunlap said to her mom as she stretched to see out the window. She really didn't mean to kick the seat. But they had been in the car FOREVER, driving all the way from Chicago to Chincoteague Island in Virginia.

Now Willa was about to miss out on the

very best part. She turned and looked out the back. All she wanted was a peek at one of the Chincoteague ponies, running on the sandy beach. She thought if she saw one, it would be a sign that moving to the island and leaving her friends behind was worth it.

Willa tried to see past the houses and across the bay but couldn't spot a thing. It was too foggy.

"We're almost home," Mom announced. "It's coming up on the left."

Willa rolled her eyes, hoping to get the attention of her little brother, Ben. He didn't like it when Mom called the new house "home," either. They didn't live there *yet*. And, as far as Willa knew, no one had lived in the old gray house in a long time. Willa thought there was a good

reason. It didn't look very "homey" in pictures.

She glanced around at the houses along the narrow street. They looked like they had been built a long time ago, but they did have lots of new flowers in the front yards. The Dunlaps had never had a yard, just a balcony in their last apartment in Chicago.

One of the houses on the street had a giant tree with a rope swing hanging from a high branch. Willa had only swung on the chain-link swings in the city parks with her best friend, Kate.

Ben had hardly said one word the whole ride. But that wasn't unusual for him. He had read through his comic collection and then napped. Willa couldn't nap. She couldn't even read one of the dozen books in her backpack. She was too anxious.

Their dad had been quiet too. He had been quiet a lot since they had decided to move. The only thing he had talked about was the new kitchen for the new restaurant they were going to open. Their parents were going to run a bed-and-breakfast, and their dad would be the head chef.

The whole family had agreed that they would call the restaurant the Family Farm. It sounded cozy and friendly. Dad liked how it hinted that they were going to try to grow some of their own food. Willa and Ben liked how it sounded as if there would be animals there. But neither Mom nor Dad had made any promises about pets.

"Yay! We're here! Our new home!" Mom made another happy announcement. Willa knew that, in many ways, this already was home for her mom. She had grown up on Chincoteague Island. She had grown up hearing the stories of the famous ponies of nearby Assateague Island.

Once the car was parked, Mom swung her door open, stepped out, and breathed in the seaside air. Willa could already smell the salt in the car. She remembered it from trips to her grandparents' house. The smell of the ocean was everywhere.

Willa jumped out of the backseat and joined her mother. She leaned back as she looked up to the roof and back down again. There was a lot of house to see: three stories; a big covered porch that wrapped around the front to the side; and lots of windows set on a sloping roof.

"You don't think it's haunted, do you?"

Willa flinched. She hadn't heard Ben come up behind her. It didn't help that he almost always spoke in a whisper.

"No," she answered, but the house was large

enough for a whole family of ghosts, plus grand-parent ghosts too. "It's just old. Mom and Dad will fix it up. You'll see."

Willa skipped to the end of the driveway and back, trying to loosen up her knees after the drive. Her parents stood in front of the house. Her dad had his hand resting on her mom's shoulder, and her mom had her arm around his waist.

"A cat!" Ben yelped.

He pointed and jogged up onto the porch. Wood planks creaked as he ran. The cat's fur was a mess of colors—brown, white, orange, and black—but its eyes were a clear, bright green.

Willa glanced at Dad and held her breath. How long until he tried to stop Ben? The cat's fur wasn't scraggly, and the animal wasn't terribly skinny, but it sure looked like a stray.

"Hey now, Ben," Dad called. "We don't know that cat."

Willa laughed. Of course they didn't know the cat.

"Don't get any ideas, buddy," Dad continued. "We have a lot of work to do around this place.

We cannot take on the responsibility of a pet right now."

What was the point of moving to a gigantic house if you couldn't have pets? Willa rushed to join Ben. She loved cats. She loved most animals. She understood what her dad was saying, but she hoped he would change his mind.

Just as Willa reached her brother, the cat jumped to the porch railing and began to lick her paw.

"I was so close," Ben said, his bangs hanging in his hazel eyes.

"Come on, you two," Dad called again. "We have to unpack this car. We don't have time to chase some stray cat."

"It isn't just any cat," a voice announced. "It's New Cat."

A barefoot kid in cutoff jeans stood in their driveway, holding a platter that was covered in shiny, silver foil. He didn't look much older than Ben.

"New Cat belongs here. She always has," the boy explained.

"Hi," Mom said. "I'm Amelia Dunlap. This is my family, Ben, Willa, and my husband, Eric."

"Hi," the boy answered, striding toward her. "I'm Chipper. My mom says, 'Welcome to Chincoteague.' She told me to give you these. You're lucky." He held out the platter. As soon as Willa and Ben's mom took it, the boy turned and ran.

Chapter 2

THE WHOLE FAMILY WATCHED CHIPPER RUN down the road.

Mom pulled back the foil from the casserole dish. "Oh, wow. Fried oysters! I'm sure of it." She breathed in the steam from the golden nuggets.

"We're going to eat *that*?" Willa asked.

Her mom nodded.

"But it's from a stranger," Ben pointed out. "You said to never eat food from strangers."

"There are no strangers on Chincoteague," their mom answered. She set the dish down on the porch stairs and took a seat. "Come on, you guys."

Their dad seemed even less sure about the mystery food. He leaned in to smell it for himself. "I'm not going to turn down homemade food," he said, "but I would rather be making dinner in my own kitchen." Willa and Ben locked eyes. There Dad went, talking about the new kitchen again.

"Oysters are seafood, aren't they?" Ben made a funny face.

"Turn up your nose all you want. It leaves more for me." Mom picked a crispy piece from

the dish. She dipped it into the creamy sauce and took a noisy bite. She closed her eyes. "Delicious," she said, reaching for another.

Dad grabbed the next-largest piece and popped it into his mouth. "I take it back," he said. "I will happily eat this over my cooking. It's fantastic."

It was not often that their dad enjoyed someone else's cooking. Sometimes a sandwich was "boring" or mashed potatoes were "too gummy." Dad had an odd way of talking about food.

Ben took a small bite. "I don't even taste the seafood," he admitted. "I don't even see the seafood." Ben cracked himself up.

The whole family took turns picking up the last crumbs of deep-fried goodness. In the open air, it felt like the start of a new adventure that they would all share. But for Willa, it changed as soon as they went inside.

The house was dusty and dim. The sun cast long shadows across the wooden floor. The ceilings were high and the rooms empty. There was a lot of space, but to Willa it didn't feel like home.

Willa's large duffel bag threw her off balance. She adjusted her grip as she started up the old, wide staircase.

"Honey, just leave everything in the main room for tonight," Mom said. "We need to clean the upstairs before we take stuff up there."

With a sigh, Willa dropped her backpack and duffel next to Ben's stuff. It didn't take her long to feel cooped up, surrounded by boxes and packed bags.

When Ben followed their parents to the back of the house, Willa slipped out the front door.

She could practically smell her way to the bay. The breeze swept in from the ocean. She followed the road they had driven on earlier until she came to a path. It was narrow and cut through the tall marsh grass.

When Willa and Ben had visited before, she had explored lots of paths with Grandma Edna, her mom's mom. Grandma Edna knew every path, every plant, and every family on Chincoteague.

Willa was surprised her grandparents hadn't

been at the house to greet them. She guessed they'd be over bright and early in the morning.

Grandma Edna and Grandpa Reed had come to see them in the city for holidays, but the Dunlaps hadn't been to visit them on the island in a few years. Spending more time with their grandparents was a good part of moving. Willa tried not to think about the bad ones.

Leaving her best friend, Kate, was one of them. What if Willa didn't make any friends here? What if it never felt like home?

The path finally led to a long dock that reached far into the water. Sitting down at the end, Willa felt just a little closer to Assateague, which was just across the bay.

Willa knew about the wild ponies there. Her mom had read her books, and Willa had

found others in the library. The most famous of the ponies was Misty. Misty had been born on Assateague, but she had ended up living with a family on Chincoteague. That was a really long time ago.

For a few months after she had read the book about Misty, Willa had lived for ponies. She had reread the books and taken horseback-riding lessons. That was before the six months of ice-skating and the year of gymnastics. Willa had read a lot about those things too, until she had found something new.

But the ponies weren't like famous ice-skaters or gymnasts. The ponies were a mystery to Willa. They lived on their own, surviving on their instincts. Part of Willa still didn't believe their stories were true.

Willa took off her sandals and dangled her legs over the side. She gazed across the bay. She wondered if the ponies on the island felt free and if—

C-r-e-a-k-k-k . . .

Willa jumped as the dock creaked behind her.

"It's beautiful, isn't it?" her mother said, and sat next to Willa. Surprisingly, she was barefoot. Willa couldn't remember the last time she had seen her mom barefoot outdoors.

Willa nodded. "Is it really true?" she asked. "The story of the wild ponies?"

"Well, there isn't any way to prove it, but I believe it is true. I believe the old stories of the Spanish ship caught in a storm, and I believe that when the ship crashed, the ponies escaped as the ship sank.

"They swam to the island of Assateague that you see right there. They learned how to live and take care of themselves in a new place. They've been surviving ever since."

Willa glanced over at her mom. She had a faraway look in her eyes. She squeezed Willa's hand.

"Anyway, we do know that Misty's story was

true," Mom said. "Dad and I have even talked about calling the bed-and-breakfast Misty Inn, because people love that story. A lot of them visit the island to see where Misty lived."

"But I thought we were calling it the Family Farm," Willa said.

"Well, that's the name of the restaurant," Mom explained. "We'll have a different name for the inn." She paused.

"It's a good thing you were here, young lady," Mom said, pushing Willa's hair behind her ear. "Because otherwise you'd be in trouble, running off like that."

"I thought you wanted us to be able to run off. You said you wanted us to explore more. Isn't that why we left the city?"

"Well, yes and no," her mom responded. "I

do want those things for you, but I also want to know where you are. And you still need to watch your brother. You know, this move won't be as easy on him."

Does she think this is easy for me? Willa wondered.

"Ben has a harder time making friends and trying new things." Her mom tried to explain. "You're always finding new hobbies. It's easier for you."

Mom reached out and squeezed Willa's hand again.

Willa knew her parents were worried about Ben, but she didn't think he needed someone around all the time, acting like a babysitter.

"Come on," Mom said, standing up. "It's time to get back." Willa put on her shoes and followed her mother. "The moving truck comes with our furniture tomorrow. So we're just going to use our sleeping bags in the main room tonight. Your dad's making popcorn."

Popcorn was a family tradition. And a family sleepover sounded like fun. And tomorrow, the real adventure would begin. At least she hoped it would.

Chapter 3

WILLA OPENED HER EYES WITH A START. Something didn't seem right.

She looked to one side. She could see her parents were both soundly sleeping in the dim morning light.

But when she turned to the other, Ben was gone. His sleeping bag was empty.

She quickly dressed, tugged her gym

shoes on, and hurried out the back door.

Where is he? Willa worried. *Mom and Dad will be so mad at me if anything happens to him.*

She was staring at the old barn. It was in the very back corner of the lot, half hidden by tall grass and ivy vines.

Willa raced to the tall double doors, which were cracked open, and stepped inside.

"Ben?" she called out. "Ben?"

"Here I am," she heard him say.

"Where?" Willa asked.

"Up here! In the hayloft," Ben answered.

She looked up and there was her brother, sitting on the edge of a platform, swinging his legs. It wasn't like her brother to go off on his own.

A knot was in Willa's stomach. What if Ben

fell? She tried to keep her voice steady.

"Ben, you have to come down. Now. We don't even know if it's safe up there."

Ben's smile turned into a frown. He hadn't thought about the hayloft being dangerous. He stood up and walked to the ladder. But when he looked down, he panicked.

"I'm not climbing down that ladder," he said. "It's too far."

"Well, you climbed *up*," Willa said angrily.

"How about that rope?" Ben said, pointing to a thick rope that hung down to the barn floor. "It looks easier than the ladder."

Willa walked over to the rope to check it out. It was a pulley system.

She pulled on it hard. It seemed pretty secure.

Ben looped one leg around the rope and kept one on the loft. His body swayed away from the platform and then . . . he lost his balance.

Ben tried to throw a leg out to grab at the loft, but he couldn't reach. He grabbed the rope harder. His knuckles grew white as he dangled in the air.

"I'm stuck," he cried. "It won't move."

Willa steadied the rope from the ground. "You have to slide down. Loosen up on the rope and ease yourself down."

"I can't," Ben whispered. His eyes were squeezed shut.

"You have to, or else you'll be hanging there all day. And I don't know if the pulley will hold that long."

Ben's hands burned as the old rope slid

through them. "Almost," Willa said. "You can just drop."

Ben paused but then let go, landing on his backside.

He stared at his hands. They were scraped and bloody, and they stung.

Ben bit his lower lip to keep from crying. He wiped his hands on the back of his pants.

Willa sat next to her brother and put her arm around his shoulder.

"You'll be okay," she said. "But next time, wake me up before you go."

From where they sat, Willa could see that the barn had different sections. "Stalls," she whispered happily to herself. Horses or ponies had probably lived there at one time. Of course, it was the *perfect* place for animals of all kinds.

Willa and Ben had never had pets in the city. Not even a fish.

Ben took a deep breath. "Is it my fault?" he said, looking up at the loft.

"What?" said Willa.

"Is it my fault that we had to move? The whole playground thing, with those older kids?"

"Don't be silly," Willa said. "Mom's wanted to move for years."

What Willa had said was true, but Ben had caught her off guard. He hadn't ever talked about the boys on the playground—the ones the teachers had warned his parents about. The ones who always teased Ben because he was so quiet.

"But Dad didn't want to move," Ben

reminded her. "Maybe he changed his mind because of me."

"Maybe he did," Willa admitted. "But it doesn't matter. We're here now."

Her words were drowned out by the sound of an engine. Willa stood up and rushed over to the barn door.

"It's Grandma and Grandpa," she called to her brother. "Come on."

Willa held her hand out to Ben, to help him stand, and they ran out to see their grandparents.

"There you are!" Grandma Edna said, opening her arms wide. Both Willa and Ben hurried over for a warm hug. She smelled sweet, like fresh hay. She wrapped one arm around each grandchild. "Can you believe we'll get to see them all the time now, Pops?"

"Nope. Still hasn't quite sunk in." Grandpa Reed waited patiently. The two kids snuggled in to him next.

"Hello!" The kids' parents waved from the porch. Mom rushed down the steps. She was already dressed in her old jeans and a long-sleeved plaid shirt. Her hair was pulled back in a low ponytail. Mom first hugged her mom. Next she leaned over Ben's head to kiss Grandpa Reed on the cheek.

"Look, there's the cat again," Ben exclaimed as he pointed to the back porch.

"Wait a minute, Ben. What happened to your hands?" Mom grabbed Ben's wrist and looked at his bloody palm.

"It's just a cut from a rope in the barn," Willa tried to explain. She gave Ben a *Don't say a word* look. Her mom glanced at the old building. "You'd better go wash those hands off."

"But the cat," Ben insisted.

"No way are you touching that cat with an open cut," Mom replied. "Eric, can you take Ben inside? The Band-Aids are in my bag."

They all watched them go inside. Grandma

Edna turned to her daughter. "You're going to need to loosen up a little, Amelia," she said. "Kids need room to breathe and solve their own problems."

"Mom, you know that's part of the reason we moved here," Mom huffed. Willa had never heard her mom and grandma argue.

"Now, you two," Grandpa Reed said after a pause. "You're both coming from the same place so don't fight. I'm coming from the place of hunger. Willa, why don't you give me a quick tour so we can head on inside and eat. Grandma made some of her strawberry scones."

Willa took her grandpa's hand. They walked toward the back of the house, and Grandma Edna followed. New Cat was right behind them. "I haven't had much time to explore yet," she confessed. "But I saw these beautiful flowers on the back fence."

Grandpa Reed looked up and nodded.

"Nasturtiums," Grandma Edna told them. "Why, they're just lovely."

"I could use those in salads." That was Dad again. He and Ben had returned. Ben had white gauze wrapped around his palms. "But we'll have to get a lawn mower to get anywhere close to them."

"Oh, a few goats could take care of that overgrown grass," Grandma suggested.

Eric coughed back a laugh. "We are starting a bed-and-breakfast, Edna, *not* a petting zoo."

Grandpa Reed broke in. "Yes, dear, we all know that you will find any excuse to surround yourself with more animals. But we all also know that it's time for breakfast." With that, he lifted Ben by the middle and swung him upside down. Ben giggled. "This boy's ready to eat. He's light as a feather. Let's plump him up."

Grandpa Reed led everyone inside. Willa walked behind. She liked the way her grandma thought. What was the point in having a big house and big yard if you didn't share it with animals? They needed at least one pet, maybe two. And the sooner the better.

Chapter 4

THEY HADN'T BEEN TO THEIR GRANDPARENTS'
house in years, but Willa had warm memories
of their little island farm. Grandma Edna, who
was a veterinarian, ran a small animal rescue center. She had taken in everything from
pet rabbits to geese to goats. And, of course,
Chincoteague ponies.

"Remember how she let us throw flakes of

hay into the pony paddock last time?" Willa asked Ben in a whisper. Her brother nodded. "You were so small, you could hardly reach over the fence."

Willa and Ben were sitting in the backseat of their grandparents' truck, on the way to their farm. Once their bikes arrived, they'd be able to visit on their own, whenever they wanted.

Ben frowned as Willa giggled. A lot had changed, and he was definitely taller now. Maybe this time he'd get to ride a pony by himself.

"They still have ponies, right?"

"I think so," Willa answered. "Mom said that Grandma's getting older and isn't taking in new animals anymore. And there's another pony rescue on the island now too."

When they turned onto the long driveway to

Miller Farm, Ben saw his sister cross her fingers. He looked past her to the fenced-in field. There, a small band of ponies came into view. They weren't the silky sleek horses like at the riding stable near the city. These ponies had muddy knees and thick, shaggy manes. They were still beautiful.

Grandpa brought the truck to a stop close to a one-story house.

"You'll have to meet the newest member of our herd," Grandma said as she swung the passenger door closed. She motioned to a horse that was nearly twice as tall as the ponies. He was all black, except his legs had long white hair from the knee down. "Jake is a Shire, a real, live draft horse. He's a bigger sweetheart than the rest combined."

"Literally," Grandpa uttered, helping Ben and Willa jump down from the backseat of the truck.

"The ponies are all moving on in age," Grandma Edna explained, motioning to the field. "They're getting more stubborn by the day. They aren't much for riding anymore. Annie pins back her ears whenever she sees a saddle. Oh, she pins her ears all the time." Grandma pointed to a chestnut mare with a star on her forehead. Willa remembered that she had ridden Annie the last time she visited Miller Farm. Well, she'd sat on Annie, and Grandma had led her around.

"Truth is," Grandma continued, "I don't have time for riding either. But Jake loves to get out and about."

Willa sighed. While there were still ponies on the farm, it sounded like they were pretty much off limits. Except for Jake, and he was so tall, Willa couldn't imagine getting on him.

"Can I pet him?" Ben asked. The horse had eased his way to the fence.

When Grandma nodded, Ben stepped forward and held out his hand. The draft horse's great tongue licked Ben's fingers. Ben laughed.

"Jake's always friendly, but the ponies are only interested if you have a treat," Grandma explained.

"They're a hungry bunch," Grandpa said.

"No more than you, Reed. It's just their nature. They're grazers. It's their job, eating enough to keep them going.

"Come on, kids. We should water the horses,"

Grandma Edna said. It was a funny term, but Willa knew they weren't going to throw water on the horses. It meant filling up the drinking trough. Grandpa went inside to make sand-wiches, and Willa helped Grandma untangle the green hose. She slid it through the fence and into the metal trough.

"Edna!" Grandpa called from the door. "Clifton left a note for you. Says a fellow named Worth called on the barn phone and is on his way over."

Grandma nodded as she worked the kinks out of the hissing hose. "Clifton's a teenager who helps out around the place," she said. "He's awful nice, and he's got a sister about your age, Willa."

Willa smiled, but she didn't have time to ask

questions. A truck and trailer began its way up the farm's long gravel drive. They all turned to look.

The truck stopped, and a man with a cowboy hat got out and shut the door. "You Edna Miller?" he asked.

"Well, yes."

"My name's Dale Worth. I got your name from a friend. She said you take in Chincoteague ponies."

Grandma opened her mouth to answer, but the man kept right on talking.

"My neighbors are going through a rough patch and need to let their pony go. I promised them I'd take care of it. So here I am, and here's the pony." He motioned to the battered trailer and moved toward its back end.

"I'm not exactly taking new animals," Grandma called out.

"I called earlier," Mr. Worth said, "but I've only got the trailer for the day, so I came ahead."

"Now's not the best time," Grandma continued. "The fence on our small paddock is broken. We have no way to separate a new animal from the herd."

The man kept moving as Grandma talked. He lifted a lever and pulled down a ramp.

Grandma had more to say, but the man disappeared inside the trailer. There was the shuffling of hooves on metal, and then a sleek buckskin backed down the ramp.

Willa held her breath. Ben's jaw dropped. Grandma Edna just stared.

The pony snorted as she stood next to Mr.

Worth. Her ears twitched. Her coat was a creamy butterscotch, and her mane and tail were the color of cocoa. Her dark eyes were warm and friendly.

"This here's Starbuck," Mr. Worth said. "She's a nice mare, but she loved her owner. I suspect she's going to be lonesome not having young Merry around."

Ben looked at Grandma. Her eyes were

steady on the pony, but it looked like she had all kinds of thoughts churning around in her head.

Willa couldn't understand why Grandma wasn't running up and hugging the pony that very second.

"She looks to be a fine horse," Grandma said, "but I don't have the paddock space now. Like I said, my other gate's broken."

Ben had heard Mom describe Grandma as "being stubborn as a mule." Why was the broken fence such a big problem?

"I can't come back. My place is more than an hour south of here, and this pony needs a home now," Mr. Worth explained.

Willa felt a tightness across her chest.

She looked at Grandma. Why was she taking so long?

Finally Grandma spoke. "Where are the papers?" she asked.

Mr. Worth hesitated. "I don't have them, but the family promised they'd send the paperwork as soon as things settle."

"This is very unusual," Grandma said, shaking her head. "Very unusual."

She took a deep breath. For the first time, her eyes looked over to her grandchildren. "What do you think, should we take this pony?"

Ben's eyes grew in size. Willa could barely speak but managed to say, "It seems like the right thing to do."

"Yes," Ben agreed.

"Very well," Grandma concluded. "I suppose we could clear out a space in the barn for the time being." She took the pony's lead and

handed it to Willa while she got contact information from Mr. Worth.

Even in the hot summer sun, Willa had
goose bumps. She reached out and smoothed
the soft hair along the mare's neck. Ben picked
a long blade of grass. He let Starbuck eat it
from his hand.

They were still standing there when Mr.
Worth backed the truck and trailer down the
drive. They were both smiling.

Chapter 5

"EDNA?"

Willa and Ben turned when Grandpa called.

"She's in the barn," Ben said.

"She said she has to figure out which stall Starbuck will go in," Willa explained.

"Starbuck?" Grandpa asked, his eyes lingering on the new pony. "Edna?" he called again.

At that moment Grandma came out of the

barn, but she didn't see Grandpa. She had a bucket of brushes in one hand and a flake of hay in the other.

"I need one of you to help move some feed bags. The other can help me groom the mare, make her feel at home. Remember how we did it when you last visited?" She stopped short when she saw Grandpa.

"I go in the house for five minutes and there's a new horse in our driveway when I come out?" He tried to hide a stubborn smile.

"It must be what Clifton's note was about. This pony needs a place to stay for a while, until I can find her a better home," Grandma explained.

"I've heard that before," said Grandpa.

"Well, I thought the timing might be right,"

Grandma replied. She raised her eyebrows and tilted her head toward Willa and Ben.

Grandpa laughed. "Your grandma might be retired," he said, "but animals still run her life."

"They keep finding me," Grandma admitted.

While Grandpa helped Grandma in the barn, Ben and Willa took turns brushing Starbuck.

The pony didn't really need brushing. She didn't have a speck of dirt on her, but she seemed to like the attention. Willa ran the currycomb in circles on her belly, and Ben petted the swirl of hair on the center of her face. "What did Grandma mean when she said 'for a while'?" Ben asked.

"I don't know," Willa said with a shrug. "Mom said that Grandma sometimes finds a

new home for the animals, the ones that don't really need to be at a rescue center."

Starbuck let out a deep sigh. So did Willa. The pony turned around to give her shirt a friendly nip. "I know, girl," Willa said. "I sure hope you get to stay here."

♥

When it was time to introduce Starbuck to her stall, the pony didn't want to budge. "Move on," Grandma said, patting the pony on the rump.

Starbuck stepped forward with slow, stiff movements. Ben walked next to Grandma, carrying the brushes. "Looks like it hurts her," he said.

Grandma looked down. "I think you're right, Ben."

They took the pony to her stall for a closer look.

"See how nice this stall is?" Willa said as she led Starbuck inside. The stall smelled of fresh sawdust.

Grandma knelt by the mare's side. She ran her hands down her leg. "Sure enough," Grandma said, "she's got heat and swelling in this leg. It could be from the trailer ride, or maybe from before. It's a good thing we have a place to keep her. I don't think she'll be ready for the paddock for a while."

Grandma told Willa and Ben that the leg wasn't too bad. "But she'll need company so she doesn't get bored in this stall. It's no fun to be cooped up on your own, is it?" Grandma scratched Starbuck on her lower lip.

"We're happy to help," Willa said eagerly.

Ben nodded. He petted the pony's muzzle, which was the softest thing he had ever felt.

Every morning Willa and Ben rode their bikes to their grandparents' farm. They did whatever chores Grandma Edna gave them—weeding the garden, cleaning the saddles, sweeping the barn. But she did warn her grandchildren. "We don't know much about this pony," she told them. "For now, no going in her stall unless I am in the barn too."

Mom and Dad were so busy with the house—the furniture had arrived and the rooms needed to be set up—that they didn't have time to take the kids around to all the local sights. "The carpenters are coming on Saturday," Mom said. "We have a lot to figure out before they arrive."

But Ben and Willa didn't care. Even though they hadn't seen or met any kids their own age—except for Chipper—they had each other.

And for once, they wanted to do the exact same thing: see Starbuck. Willa couldn't believe that for the past few days, she hadn't thought about Chicago or Kate once. She had Starbuck to thank.

Chapter 6

ONE MORNING, THE SMELL OF BANANA BREAD
woke both kids and they hurried downstairs.
They had been on the island almost a week, and
this was the first homemade breakfast. "This is
really good, Mom," Willa said. Their dad was a
chef, but Mom was the baker.

"I need you two to do me a favor." Mom was
holding a casserole dish with an envelope taped

inside. "We need to return this. I did some detective work, and Chipper is one of the Starling kids. They also have an older girl. They live up the road."

By "detective work," Willa knew that her mom had talked to Grandma Edna. They hadn't seen Chipper since that first night. And now Mom probably wanted them to make friends with the Starling kids.

"Do I have to go too?" Ben asked.

"Yes, you do," Mom said. "I hear that the Starlings have something new in their backyard that you'll be interested in."

When they were a few yards from the porch, Mom opened the door. "I invited them to a picnic at our house," she called out. "After the construction's done. Just so you know."

Willa smiled at Ben. Mom *loved* picnics. Even though they had a huge house now, she would rather plan a gathering outside.

"I wonder what the surprise is," Willa said, gripping the dish in both hands. "Maybe a trampoline."

"Or a pool," Ben offered.

When they came to the house, Willa realized it was one she had noticed when they first moved in. There was a swing hanging from a large tree, bikes on the lawn, and wildflowers.

The doorbell was under a hand-painted plaque with the words, WELCOME TO OUR HOUSE. HOPE YOU FEEL AT HOME. Willa pushed the bell and waited. A happy scream came from the backyard. "Maybe it *is* a pool," Willa whispered.

The door opened. A woman who was not much taller than Willa greeted them. She had short almond-brown hair and big blue-rimmed glasses that made her look like a librarian in an old book.

"We're returning this," Willa said. She handed the dish over.

"You must be the Dunlaps," the woman said. "Willa and Ben, right? Your grandma has told me all about you. Sorry my kids haven't been over. They've been busy. I can't get them to leave the backyard."

"It's okay," Willa said. "We've been busy too. Thank you for the oysters. They were delicious."

"My dad would really like the recipe," added Ben.

"Ben," Willa said, "you can't just ask some-one for the recipe."

"Well," Mrs. Starling said, taking the dish in her hands. "I'll have to think about that. It is an old family secret." She smiled like a helpful librarian too.

Willa and Ben followed her through the house. Books and wooden ducks were every-where. When they came to a sliding glass door, she opened it. "Chipper! Sarah! The Dunlaps are here."

Two kids looked up from where they sat on a plaid blanket. Ben looked at Willa—it definitely was not a pool.

"Why don't you show them the puppies?" Mrs. Starling said. "Just keep it down. Bess is napping," she reminded them.

"Bess is our little sister," Chipper explained once Willa and Ben reached the blanket. "We have a big sister too. Kat."

"Katherine," Sarah corrected. She smoothed out her dark shiny hair, then her skirt. "We just got Marnie about a couple of months ago," she continued. "We didn't know she was pregnant."

Chipper pointed to the black and white pups. "That's Amos, Ranker, Bella, Dolly, Rice Cake, Tramp, and Jubilee," he said, rattling off their names.

"They were born just before you moved in," he added. "They'll stay with Marnie for a few months. But then we have to give them away."

"All but one," Sarah added.

Ben reached out to lift Rice Cake, but the puppy squirmed and Ben dropped him.

"What did you just do?" Sarah cried. "You could have hurt him!"

Willa looked at her brother. His eyes filled with tears.

"It was a mistake," she said to Sarah. "He didn't mean to hurt Rice Cake."

Sarah frowned. "I think you should leave. *Now.*"

Willa and Ben quickly stood up and turned to go. But Chipper stopped them.

"I have to bring my father his lunch," he said. "Want to come along for the ride?"

"Sure," answered Willa. She and Ben turned to go back into the house, but Chipper headed to the other side of the yard, toward a long wooden walkway that led to a short dock.

"We're taking a boat?" she asked.

"It's just a skiff. It's okay," Chipper said. "I'm a good driver." Chipper handed them life jackets and leaned down to untie the boat.

Once she was buckled, Willa stepped into the front of the skiff. Her whole body wavered as the boat sloshed underneath her. She quickly sat down. "Hold on tightly, Ben," Willa warned her brother.

Ben watched his sister from the dock. He fiddled with his straps. Ben wondered if this was allowed. What would Mom say? They were getting in a boat with a stranger—and that stranger was a kid! Chipper finished untying the boat.

Ben glanced at his sister's back, took a deep breath, and stepped in.

"My dad's a fisherman," Chipper said, once they were on their way. "He takes people on fishing cruises. We've got to get there before they leave." As the motor revved, the front of the small boat lifted out of the water. Willa grabbed on to her seat. The boat made its way out of a small creek into the open bay.

"So, you probably know that Assateague is over there, with the wild ponies," Chipper told them after a while. "And this is about where the ponies come across on swim day."

Willa and Ben both looked from one shore to the other. The white sands of Assateague looked far from the marshy banks of Chincoteague. The ponies swam it every year, even the new colts. Then many of the youngest ponies would go up to auction the next day. It was how Chincoteague's Volunteer Fire Department kept track of the herd. They needed to keep it from getting too big. Assateague was a small island. Only so many ponies could live there.

Willa couldn't help thinking of Starbuck. Ben couldn't either. Mr. Worth had said she was a *real* Chincoteague pony. Had she swum the full length of the bay when she was a foal? What was her story?

Had Starbuck been born on Assateague, as wild as the sea?

Willa let the salty air fill her lungs. She decided it was okay if Sarah didn't want to be friends. Her brother, Chipper, still seemed nice.

But he would be a better friend for Ben than for her.

Willa clung to the hope that Grandma wouldn't find a home for Starbuck. As long as she could be with Starbuck, she could be happy. Still, she knew it wasn't the same as having a friend. She tried pushing that thought out of her head, but it stayed with her all the way to dropping off lunch, and even after she and Ben returned home to Misty Inn.

Chapter 7

Dear Kate,

I miss you so, so, so much.

How is camp? Tell me some
of the new stuff you learned on
the computer.

It is so different here in Chincoteague. This morning chickens
woke Ben and me up.

Then this woman, Mrs. Cornett, who was wearing red boots and a yellow poncho, came out of nowhere and said they were hers. We did help her bring her chickens home, but how strange is that?

I've only met one girl, and we are already not friends.

My grandma and grandpa have a really nice farm with lots of horses. Ben and I go there every day, and we're taking care of a pony named Starbuck.

My parents still won't let us have a pet, but there is a cat here.

I've decided that Ben and I are going to try to make a fort in the barn that's in the back of our house. There's a lot of gross, old stuff in it, like rusty coffee cans, but I did find a bowl that says "Woof" in the bottom.

I sure wish you were here with me to help us build it.

Love,

Willa

Chapter 8

EARLY EVERY MORNING WILLA AND BEN WOULD go to the barn and spend time building their fort. They had already cleaned up the hayloft and thrown out a huge pile of junk.

But they couldn't wait to see Starbuck each day. And she seemed pleased to see them.

The buckskin pony had grown used to them. Grandma Edna had noticed. She now allowed her grandchildren to go in and out of Starbuck's stall as if the pony were their own.

One day Grandma had a surprise for Willa and Ben when they arrived at the farm.

"You've both been working hard. It's about time you got to take a ride," she said. In a few minutes, they were both saddled up.

Willa was in front on Maude, a steady pinto. Ben was on the great Jake. Grandma Edna walked on foot, staying close by Ben's side.

"He's like a big easy chair," Grandma said, glancing up at Ben. "You can't fall off. He's too wide."

As Ben eased forward and back with Jake's every step, he thought it was closer to sitting in a rocking chair—a rocking chair on the beach. From Jake's back, Ben had a fine view of the farm. He could almost see out to the ocean.

"Isn't it windy on Assateague?" Ben asked. "What about winter? Don't the horses get cold?"

Grandma Edna paused. "Well, yes, I'm sure they do. But those ponies are tough. They've learned to take care of themselves. And nature gives them heavier coats when it gets cold."

"I don't think Starbuck would do so well over there," Ben said.

"Well, she's been pampered," Grandma replied. "She probably had a heavier coat in the winter, but her old owner groomed it away in spring. And you and Willa have brushed that pony to no end."

It was true. When they weren't wrapping

her leg or adding fresh sawdust to her stall, they had a mane comb, currycomb, or brisk brush in hand. Starbuck loved the attention. She would turn her head and watch Willa and Ben with her warm brown eyes.

"Starbuck is the best friend we've made, Grandma. We need to take care of her." Ben sounded sincere.

Willa turned around in her saddle again. Sometimes Ben surprised her. "I think you're right," Willa said. "Grandma, why do you think her old owner gave up Starbuck?"

"I'm not really sure, honey. Mr. Worth said we'd get more information soon. When we do, I'll let you know," Grandma answered.

Back at the barn, Starbuck was waiting for them. She nickered a low greeting when Willa and Ben carried in their saddles. "I wonder if we'll ever get to ride *her*," Ben said, almost to himself.

"It depends," Willa said. "Grandma might still be looking for another home for her. And she doesn't want us to grow too attached."

"But we're already attached, Willa," said Ben.

At that moment Grandma came into the barn and hung up Jake's oversize bridle next to the much smaller ones that fit the ponies. "I'm a little worried about your girl, Starbuck. She needs to get outside, but she's not ready to be in the paddock. The other horses have been together for a long time. They are not always friendly with newcomers."

Grandma had already explained to them that they used to have two paddocks. With two spaces, a new horse could go in one, and the older horses would stay in the other. They could slowly get used to one another. There were always one or two horses that liked to be in charge, and they would want to show the new horse who was boss. Grandma called it "herd dynamics."

"She needs fresh air," Grandma said, leaning down to run her hand over Starbuck's sore leg. "She's almost mended. Can't keep her cooped up much longer. Maybe you two could take her out for some grass?"

It felt like a whole new world, getting to take Starbuck out of the stall. They took her for a short walk along the far edge of the farm. The pony drew in deep breaths of air, her nostrils quivering. As pretty as she was in the barn, she seemed even more beautiful out in the open.

At Grandma's advice, they did not go far. They found a good patch of grass near the paddock fence and Starbuck happily ate.

All at once, the pony lifted her head. Her ears pricked toward a faraway sound. She called out in a high whinny.

From the far corner of the pasture, Annie's head rose. The older mare's ears pressed back against her neck. Starbuck neighed again. Annie's eyes flashed white with anger. She stretched out her neck and began to charge. She pounded across the grassy paddock, aiming right for Starbuck!

Ben scrambled up from the ground where he was sitting. Willa gripped Starbuck's halter and backed her away.

Annie's hooves skidded in the dirt when she reached the high fence. She snorted, her teeth bared.

"That's not very nice," Willa scolded the older pony. Starbuck stood behind her, rubbing her head against Willa's back. "We should probably find someplace else."

Annie stayed by the fence, eyeing the newcomer. "I don't like the way she looks at Starbuck," Ben said. He scrunched up his face at the chestnut pony.

Willa tugged at the lead line, but Starbuck wouldn't move. Even though the pony turned her head toward Willa, her hooves stayed put. "She doesn't want to go," Ben said.

"She's got to. She can't stay here," Willa said.

Ben rubbed his lips together, looking at the pony's warm eyes and alert ears. He walked over and leaned against Starbuck's backside, giving her a nudge. "It's okay, girl," he murmured.

The three of them headed toward the barn. Grandma helped put Starbuck back in her stall and then asked, "How would you both like to get some ice cream?"

Ben and Willa piled in the backseat of the truck. Willa wondered if the ice cream on Chincoteague was as good as the ice cream at Blue Hills in Chicago.

When they pulled up to the stand, Willa didn't want to get out of the truck.

Sarah Starling and her little sister, Bess, were there with their mother.

"Come on, Willa," Grandma said. "There's a long line and I'm hungry."

She smiled.

Grandma and Mrs. Starling said hello and talked about the upcoming Dunlap picnic. But Sarah didn't say *one* word to Willa—or to Ben. She just glared at them and played with the seam on her skirt. Luckily, it was not long before she left with her sister and mother.

Ben ordered a double scoop of chocolate, Grandma had butter pecan, and Willa had strawberry with sprinkles. The ice cream was yummy, but it didn't keep Willa from feeling a little bit sick to her stomach: What was going to happen when Sarah and her entire family came to the Dunlaps' next week? It could only be disaster.

Chapter 9

THE NEXT MORNING WILLA COULD HARDLY MOVE.

"Why am I so sore?" Willa complained to her mother. "I've ridden horses before." She squatted down, then stood up and shook out her legs.

"Your muscles aren't used to it. It's been a long time since you took lessons," Mom reminded Willa. She paused and looked at the measuring tape. They were in the third-floor bedroom. It was going to be part of the bed-and-breakfast, and the windows needed new curtains. Willa held one end of the tape to the corner of the window frame.

Her mom was right. It had been a long time since she had taken lessons. Willa wondered what it would be like if she hadn't given up horseback riding. She had learned a lot in the months she had taken lessons in Chicago. She knew how to be calm around horses, how to brush in the direction that the hair grew, and how to place her hand on a horse's side or rump to let it know where she was in the stall. The riding trainer had taught her all those things.

Between leg stretches, Mom asked, "Wasn't

Four Corners the best ice cream you've ever had? How was Ben when you were there? Did he say much?"

Of course Mom was more concerned about Ben. He still didn't say much, but that was Ben.

Before Willa could answer Mom's question, or tell her about mean Sarah Starling, a loud howl came from downstairs.

"It's Dad," Willa said. "It sounds like he's in pain." They dropped the tape and raced down the stairs, to the kitchen.

"Are you okay?" gasped Mom.

Dad was standing in the center of the room holding a broom over his head. He was slowly turning in circles, his gaze on the ground. Ben was sitting on the new wooden counter. He was as quiet as ever but had a huge smile on his face.

Without looking up, Dad said, "I saw a mouse. No, not just one. Two."

"Mice," Ben said.

A sigh of relief came from Mom. "You screamed so loud. I thought you'd cut off your hand!" Mom started laughing.

Dad was still spinning around. He was now holding the broom like a hatchet. "This isn't funny," he declared.

"We've had mice before," Willa pointed out. "We had them every spring in the city."

"But that was in our home," Dad reminded them. "This is also supposed to be a restaurant. The health inspectors will never approve a kitchen with mice!" Dad said.

"Traps never work, and I refuse to put out poison."

"Well, there is a simple solution," Mom began.

Listening to Mom, Ben's eyes grew wide.

Willa's heart bounced. Was Mom saying what they thought she was saying?

"All right." Dad gave in. "Go find that cat."

New Cat proved to be a good mouser. They never saw her actually catch a mouse, but she was always sniffing around the kitchen and standing guard. She would stare at the cabinets for hours, tail swishing, and would not leave her post. It took only a couple of days and the mice were gone.

"It's like all the mice packed up and left once they realized she was here," Dad said.

"They'll leave if they smell a cat," Mom said. "There are plenty of other, safer places for a mouse family to live around here."

Dad reached down and gave New Cat a

stroke from head to tail. "I appreciate a pet that can earn its keep."

Ben and Willa appreciated New Cat too. She was their first real pet, after all. Early on, the cat did not leave the kitchen. But after a couple of days—and no more signs of mice— she wandered into the family room.

Ben liked to scratch her under the chin, where her creamy white fur was soft. Willa gave her pets along the back. When New Cat was off duty, she enjoyed napping in a sunny window.

Every morning she would follow Willa and Ben to the barn, and watch them clean and sweep and move hay from one end of the space to the other. Even though they would have loved a horse, New Cat was a nice start.

Chapter 10

WILLA THOUGHT THAT TIME MOVED MORE slowly on Chincoteague. But before she knew it, it was the Friday of the family picnic. The Dunlaps were in the kitchen bright and early. Willa was helping Dad with the potato salad. Ben was helping Mom with the sugar cookies.

Mom seemed nervous.

"The first party in a new house is never

easy," she said, her head inside the pantry.

"It's not just a new house," Dad added, chopping a celery stalk. "It's also a new kitchen."

It was a new kitchen, but the fancy new stove did not fit in its space between the cabinets. The dishwasher was still in the box, so there was lots of dish and glass washing every day.

At around eleven, Mom told the kids, "Your dad and I have a lot to do. Maybe you want to ride your bikes to your grandparents' for a while? But please be home by three to help set up."

As they neared Miller Farm, they heard a high, shrill whinny. Another followed it. "Starbuck!" Willa called out. They were still at the bottom of the gravel driveway. They couldn't see the paddock. A third whinny rang out. The cry didn't sound like it could come from the calm mare with the soft brown eyes, but Ben agreed with Willa. He was sure it was Starbuck too.

Willa reached the top of the driveway first. Ben threw down his bike and ran to catch up with her. They joined Grandpa, who was already at the paddock gate. They all looked to the far side of the pasture to where Starbuck and Annie were facing off.

"What happened?" Willa asked.

"Well, I let Starbuck out," Grandpa said. "She was kicking in her stall. I thought she'd knock the barn down. Seemed like the best thing was to let her stretch her legs."

"But she was hurt, Grandpa," Willa said.

"Your grandma said she was better. I just

assumed that meant she was all right for the pasture."

Ben gripped the fence. He was listening, but he didn't take his eyes off the ponies. Starbuck's eyes flashed and her nostrils flared. There had to be something he could do.

"Where is Grandma?" Willa asked, looking around hopefully.

"Went into town. Had to go shopping before your folks' picnic." Grandpa took a handkerchief from his back pocket. He wiped his forehead.

Willa turned back to the paddock. Annie and Starbuck both had their ears pinned back. Annie took a step forward and stuck her neck out, her teeth bared. Starbuck stood her ground. "We have to get her out of there," Willa insisted. "Who knows what Annie will do."

"Annie's trying to show Starbuck who's boss," Grandpa said. "I think I know how to distract her. Annie doesn't think with her head. She thinks with her stomach.

"Willa, you come with me. Bring that pail. Ben, you keep watch," Grandpa directed. "Call us if they get any closer. Got it, bud?"

Ben nodded, his hands still tight on the

fence. Grandpa and Willa jogged toward the back of the house.

Annie inched forward, kicking up dust. The other horses kept their distance. Even Jake stayed near the gate. Starbuck didn't bare her teeth, but she also didn't back down. Annie came at her from the side and nipped her neck.

Starbuck squealed. Annie stamped and tried to back her into the fence. Starbuck skidded away. When Annie lunged, Starbuck swung around to face the older pony again. Starbuck's front leg shot up and she slammed her hoof to the ground.

"Leave her alone," Ben called out. He let go of the fence. "Get away! Starbuck didn't do anything." He heard muffled yells from Grandpa and Willa behind him, but he didn't care. Before

Ben knew it, he had unlatched the paddock gate and was walking quickly toward the two mares.

"No, you don't," Grandpa huffed, and rushed forward. He grabbed Ben by the arm. "You can't go in there, not with the horses acting like that." Grandpa tugged Ben out of the paddock. Willa locked the gate.

"But she won't leave Starbuck alone!" Ben looked at the ponies again. Their eyes were still fierce and their ears were still pinned. "She didn't do anything," he said, starting to cry.

"Don't you worry. We can get her out of there," Grandpa said, leaning down and looking Ben square in the eye. "But we have to get Annie away first. I made the mistake. I shouldn't have put Starbuck out there yet. The horses need more time to figure it out."

He stood up, his hand resting on Ben's back. "If you want to help her, how about you and Willa get that grouch Annie to take some carrots." Grandpa pointed Ben in the right direction and put a few carrots in his hands.

It was as easy as Grandpa said it would be. Annie lost all interest in Starbuck when she saw the fresh carrots dangled over the fence. The chestnut mare's ears pricked forward, and she didn't look like a cranky bully anymore.

She walked toward the kids. They carefully held out the carrots, one at a time, and Grandpa led Starbuck from the paddock. Then he locked the gate.

By the time Grandma came home, everything was back to normal. She was upset at first, but then put Grandpa to work right away, fixing the fence for the second field. That field would not only give Starbuck a place to graze, but it would let her get to know the other horses before they shared a paddock.

Willa and Ben let Starbuck eat grass behind the barn until the sun was high in the sky. Even then, it was hard putting her back in the stall.

"Grandpa's still working on the fence," Willa said. "When he's done, Starbuck can stay outside all she wants."

Willa turned to Ben and looked him in the eye. "You have to promise me you won't do anything like that again. I know you can take care of yourself, but you have to remember we're a team. We need to look out for each other."

"I know, Willa. I know," Ben said, and he meant it.

Chapter 11

"ARE YOU OKAY?" MOM ASKED, HUGGING BOTH Ben and Willa as they got out of their grandparents' truck. She grasped Ben by both shoulders. "What were you thinking?"

All the way home, sitting in the back of her grandparents' truck, Willa worried what her parents would do. They already knew about the paddock incident. Grandpa had called as soon as everyone was safe and sound.

"Amelia, your dad and I have already talked to them," Grandma explained. "Ben especially understands that he has to use his head around horses. Don't you?"

Ben nodded. He pressed his lips together. His parents were both looking at him with concern.

"I had to do it," Ben blurted. "I didn't want to stand there and watch Annie push Starbuck around. Annie was being mean. I just wanted to help Starbuck."

Now the whole family was looking at Ben in a new way.

"I understand why it was wrong. It was dangerous," he said, his words steady and clear. "I won't do it again."

Mom swept her hand over Ben's head and pulled him close. "I know," she said. "That pony is lucky to have you looking out for her."

"The kids are good with the new pony," Grandma said after a moment. "They've still got a lot to learn, but she trusts them." She smiled at Willa, who was holding Dad's hand. "Starbuck will be just fine. It takes time to get used to a new place and new horses."

They all seemed to take a deep breath, and then Dad looked around. "Speaking of new places, we're about to have company. We still have lots to do."

Ben carried two loaves of strawberry bread from Grandma's car. Willa helped her mom spread a tablecloth on the floor of the deck. "We still need outdoor furniture, but this will work for now," Mom said.

When Mom and Dad and the house were just about ready, Grandma called to Willa and Ben. "Come to the front porch," she said. The kids followed, and she handed a letter to Willa. "This came today in the mail."

As Willa pulled out the letter and started reading aloud, she realized it was from Starbuck's former owner.

Dear Mrs. Miller,

Thank you for taking care of my Starbuck. Mr. Worth told me that you seem exceptionally nice and that Starbuck will be happy on your farm. Sorry I didn't come to drop her off. It was hard for me. My family's moving for my dad's job, and Starbuck can't come. It won't feel like home without her.

I've sent her papers. She's a real Chincoteague pony. We got her at the auction when I was eight. I don't have any proof, but I like to think she could be related to Misty. You know, the pony from the famous book? When Starbuck raises her head and the wind blows through her mane, she looks like real royalty.

Please take care of Starbuck. She loves to be outside, get brushed, and be ridden bareback.

Maybe someday I can come back and visit her.

With kind thanks,

Merry Meadows

Next, they unfolded the certificate and let it all sink in. Starbuck was a *real* Chincoteague pony, born in the wild on Assateague.

After a few moments of quiet, Willa carefully folded the papers and slid them back in the envelope.

Willa had never seen Ben look so happy. Ben had never seen his sister look so happy.

"I'll bet Grandma will never give her away now," Ben said.

"I hope you're right," Willa answered.

♥

The hens, although not invited, were the first to arrive. They squawked as they made their way to the back corner of the yard.

Next, Mrs. Starling peeked around the corner with her blue-rimmed glasses. Mr. Starling came close behind. Bess was on his back.

"Hey! Where's Ben?" Chipper called out. He was still barefoot, but he was far less shy than when they met him the first day. Sarah and their big sister, Katherine, were several steps away.

"Hello!" Mom said, getting up. "Thanks so much for coming."

Mrs. Starling was carrying the same casserole dish that the oysters had been in. "Let's get that to the kitchen," Mom said. "It's time to eat!"

There was a full spread on the island in the kitchen. Mrs. Cornett, the owner of the chickens, brought egg salad and deviled eggs. There was a fresh platter of Mrs. Starling's fried oysters. Dad pulled a big batch of macaroni and cheese from the oven.

"Did you get the new stove to fit?" Grandpa asked, looking around at the changes.

"No," confessed Dad, "but this old one is pretty good. We'll keep it until it conks out. Maybe we don't need a new one after all. We'll see when the inn opens in September."

People spread out to eat—some outside on the deck. Inside, guests sat at the long table.

The kids all sat together and ate faster than the adults. Chipper was telling Ben about the puppies, but Sarah paid more attention to her potato salad than she did to Willa.

When Ben was done eating, he asked Chipper, "Want to go in the barn? Willa and I are making it into a fort."

Willa followed the boys, and once they were in the barn, Chipper and Ben were knee deep in the straw pile. Willa climbed up to the hayloft and opened up the wooden window. She was thinking about Starbuck and how much she still missed Kate when she heard someone climbing up the ladder.

It was *Sarah*!

"This could be an awesome fort," she said quietly.

Willa couldn't believe Sarah was talking to her. She especially couldn't believe Sarah had climbed the old ladder in her sundress.

"You know, Willa," Sarah continued, "I'm sorry I wasn't very nice to you the first day. And then when we saw you at Four Corners."

Sarah sat down next to Willa. At first she didn't say anything, and then she said, "There was another family that lived here for a while before you. They were from the city too. There was a girl our age." She paused and looked up at Willa, then focused on her hands again. "They only lived here for a month before heading back. I thought you all would leave too."

At once, Willa realized what Sarah was saying. Building a friendship would take trust and time. "If you're worried that we're going to move, don't be. My parents just ordered the sign for the bed-and-breakfast, and my

grandparents are here," Willa explained. She counted the reasons why they would stay on her fingers. "My mom's going to help me plant a bunch of herbs soon, and we've adopted New Cat. We're not going anywhere. And," she said, "we just found out that a new pony at my grandma's is a *real* Chincoteague pony! Just like Misty!"

"Really?" Sarah asked. "That's awesome, Willa. Do you think I can go with you one day?"

Willa nodded. "Maybe tomorrow. I'll have to ask my grandma."

Things were slowly starting to come together.

"Hey, Ben. Chipper. Come on up to the loft. You have to see this!" she called down.

The boys climbed up, and all four kids gazed out the loft window, which looked out to the bay.

Down in the yard, Bess Starling was chasing New Cat.

New Cat was chasing Mrs. Cornett's chickens.

Mrs. Cornett's chickens were chasing one another.

All the adults were eating dessert and laughing.

Chipper yelled out, "Save some cake for me."

Then he looked over at Willa and Ben and said, "I'm glad you guys moved here."

And for the first time since they arrived in Chincoteague, Willa and Ben felt exactly the same way.

ACKNOWLEDGMENTS

Thanks to everyone who helped make this book happen. Karen Nagel is as wonderful an editor as a friend, and that's saying something. Fiona Simpson grants free laughs, books, cat stories, and advice. The rest of the Aladdin team is just as generous and talented. Thanks to Mara Anastas and Kayley Hoffman, and to Laura Lyn DiSiena for the book's lovely design. Tremendous gratitude to Serena Geddes for illustrating the characters with such pluck and charm. Going way back, I offer my parents extreme appreciation for nurturing my love of horses in every way. And all my childhood affection to my pony, Moochie, and my horse, Wendy, who took that love and ran with it.

ABOUT THE SERIES

Marguerite Henry's Misty Inn series is inspired by the award-winning books by Marguerite Henry, the beloved author of such classic horse stories as *King of the Wind*; *Misty of Chincoteague*; *Justin Morgan Had a Horse*; *Stormy, Misty's Foal*; *Misty's Twilight*, and *Album of Horses*, among many other titles.

Learn more about the world of Marguerite Henry at www.MistyofChincoteague.com.